Baa Baa
Black Sheep

Baa Baa Black Sheep

As told and illustrated by
Iza Trapani

Charlesbridge

Published by Charlesbridge
85 Main Street
Watertown, MA 02472
(617) 926-0329
www.charlesbridge.com

Library of Congress Cataloging-in-Publication Data

Trapani, Iza.
Baa baa black sheep / Iza Trapani ; illustrated by Iza Trapani.
p. cm.
Summary: In this expanded version of the traditional nursery rhyme,
the black sheep has a surprise for the other farm animals.

ISBN-13: 978-1-58089-070-0; ISBN-10: 1-58089-070-9 (reinforced for library use)
ISBN-13: 978-1-58089-071-7; ISBN-10: 1-58089-071-7 (softcover)
1. Nursery rhymes. 2. Children's poetry. [1. Nursery rhymes.] I. Title.
PZ8.3.T686 Baab 2001
398.8—dc21
[E]   00-043843

Printed in China
(hc) 10 9 8 7 6 5 4 3
(sc) 10 9 8 7 6 - -

The illustrations in this book were done in watercolors on
Arches 300 lb. cold press watercolor paper.
The display type and text type were set in Quaint and 15 point Tiffany Medium.
Book production by *The Kids at Our House*
Designed by *The Kids at Our House*

For sweet Celia with love

Baa, baa, black sheep, have you any wool?
Yes sir, yes sir, three bags full.
One for the master, one for the dame,
One for the little boy who lives down the lane.
Baa, baa, black sheep, have you any wool?
Yes sir, yes sir, three bags full.

Baa, baa, black sheep, have you any milk?
Creamy, cold, and smooth as silk?
We spilled our milk—now what will we do?
Please fill our cups and we'll purr for you.

Goodness no, my shelves are very bare.
No sir, no sir, none in there.

Baa, baa, black sheep, have you any slop?
I've just finished my last drop.
I'll waste away if I don't eat soon.
One nibble ought to hold me till noon.

Silly pig, there is no slop in sight.
No sir, no sir, not one bite.

Baa, baa, black sheep, have you any hay?
Name your price and I will pay.
I'd like to buy two bales, maybe three.
I'll get the money—just wait and see.

No, I don't have any hay for sale.
No sir, no sir, not one bale.

Baa, baa, black sheep, have you any bones?
How my hungry belly groans.
Dogs cannot live on dry food alone.
Oh, won't you please just toss me a bone.

Heavens, no! I have no bones for you.
No sir, no sir, none to chew.

Baa, baa, black sheep, have you any seed?
Kindly help a friend in need.
Early this morning squirrels came by.
Knocked down my feeder, ate my supply.

No, I don't have any seed, my dear.
No sir, no sir, none in here.

Baa, baa, black sheep, have you any cheese?
May I have some pretty please?
Crackers taste yucky after a while,
A hunk of Swiss would sure make me smile.

No, I don't have cheese of any kind.
No sir, no sir, none you'll find.

Baa, baa, black sheep, won't you tell us why
"No" is always your reply?
A little kindness you've never shown.
Too mean to give a poor dog a bone.
Knit all day is all you ever do.
Boo, boo, black sheep, shame on you!

Baa, baa, black sheep, what a great surprise!
We can not believe our eyes.
We all assumed that you didn't care,
That you were selfish and wouldn't share.
Now we see and, wow, are we impressed!
You gave that which you give best!

Baa, baa, black sheep, have you any wool?
Yes sir, yes sir, three bags full.
When we have something special to give
We'll share with friends as long as we live.
Baa, baa, black sheep, have you any wool?
Yes sir, yes sir, three bags full.

Baa Baa Black Sheep

Baa, baa, black sheep, have you an-y wool? Yes sir, yes sir, three bags full.

One for the mas-ter, one for the dame, One for the lit-tle boy who lives down the lane.

Baa, baa, black sheep, have you an-y wool? Yes sir, yes sir, three bags full.

2. Baa, baa, black sheep, have you any milk?
Creamy, cold, and smooth as silk?
We spilled our milk—now what will we do?
Please fill our cups and we'll purr for you.
Goodness no, my shelves are very bare.
No sir, no sir, none in there.

3. Baa, baa, black sheep, have you any slop?
I've just finished my last drop.
I'll waste away if I don't eat soon.
One nibble ought to hold me till noon.
Silly pig, there is no slop in sight.
No sir, no sir, not one bite.

4. Baa, baa, black sheep, have you any hay?
Name your price and I will pay.
I'd like to buy two bales, maybe three.
I'll get the money—just wait and see.
No, I don't have any hay for sale.
No sir, no sir, not one bale.

5. Baa, baa, black sheep, have you any bones?
How my hungry belly groans.
Dogs cannot live on dry food alone.
Oh, won't you please just toss me a bone.
Heavens, no! I have no bones for you.
No sir, no sir, none to chew.

6. Baa, baa, black sheep, have you any seed?
Kindly help a friend in need.
Early this morning squirrels came by.
Knocked down my feeder, ate my supply.
No, I don't have any seed, my dear.
No sir, no sir, none in here.

7. Baa, baa, black sheep, have you any cheese?
May I have some pretty please?
Crackers taste yucky after a while,
A hunk of Swiss would sure make me smile.
No, I don't have cheese of any kind.
No sir, no sir, none you'll find.

8. Baa, baa, black sheep, won't you tell us why
"No" is always your reply?
A little kindness you've never shown.
Too mean to give a poor dog a bone.
Knit all day is all you ever do.
Boo, boo, black sheep, shame on you!

9. Baa, baa, black sheep, what a great surprise!
We can not believe our eyes.
We all assumed that you didn't care,
That you were selfish and wouldn't share.
Now we see and, wow, are we impressed!
You gave that which you give best!

10. Baa, baa, black sheep, have you any wool?
Yes sir, yes sir, three bags full.
When we have something special to give
We'll share with friends as long as we live.
Baa, baa, black sheep, have you any wool?
Yes sir, yes sir, three bags full.